THE THREE LITTLE PIGS

A Story About Patience

Library of Congress Cataloging-in-Publication Data
Names: Rusu, Meredith, adapter. | Hughes, Beth, illustrator.
Title: The three little pigs : a story about patience / adapted by Meredith Rusu ; illustrated by Beth Hughes.
Description: New York : Children's Press, an imprint of Scholastic 2020. | Series: Tales to grow by | Audience: Grades 4-6. | Summary: A retelling of the classic story emphasizing the importance of patience and careful planning. Contains questions and guidelines for parents and educators.
Identifiers: LCCN 2019033823 | ISBN 9780531231890 (library binding) | ISBN 9780531246238 (paperback)
Subjects: LCSH: Three little pigs--Adaptations. | Swine--Folklore. | Patience--Juvenile fiction. | Fairy tales. | Folklore. | CYAC: Folklore. | Pigs--Folklore. | Patience--Folklore. | LCGFT: Fairy tales.
Classification: LCC PZ8.1.R884 Th 2020 | DDC 398.2 [E]--dc23

Design by Book & Look

Printed in North Mankato, MN, USA 113

1 2 3 4 5 6 7 8 9 10 R 29 28 27 26 25 24 23 22 21 20

Scholastic Inc., 557 Broadway, New York, NY 10012

THE THREE LITTLE PIGS

A Story About Patience

Includes expert advice on how to encourage patience!

Adapted by
Meredith Rusu

Illustrated by
Beth Hughes

Expert advice by
Eva Martínez

Children's Press®
An Imprint of Scholastic Inc.

Once, there were three little pigs who lived with their mother in a tiny cottage. Their mother loved them very much, and she tried her best to teach them all the important things in life, like kindness, hard work, and patience.

But sometimes, the two younger piggies had a hard time paying attention....

Have you ever
had trouble paying attention
to something? What are some
activities you like paying
attention to?

The littlest one was silly and carefree. He would play all day, poking hedgehogs with sticks while they were napping just to see them curl up into little balls.

And the middle piggy was rather lazy. When their mother would ask for help stirring the soup for dinner, he would always say he was too busy watching for shapes in the clouds.

But the oldest piggy was polite and thoughtful. He'd build gadgets to help around the cottage, and he was so patient while he worked that his brothers would make fun of him.

"You're growing moss on your snout!" the youngest would tease.

"If you would just finish quickly, you could play with us," the middle brother would add.

But their older brother just smiled. "Important things are worth being patient for."

One morning, their mother said to them, “You have all grown into such big piggies now. This cottage has become too small. It is time for you to go make your own homes. Work hard and be patient, and your homes will be sturdy and strong.”

So the pigs kissed their mother goodbye, promising to do as she said.

But as soon as they had left, the youngest little piggy moaned. “It's so boring building houses. I want to play!”

He gathered some straw and threw together a wobbly shack as quickly as he could. Then, he went back to chasing hedgehogs.

Seeing his brother finish so quickly made the middle piggy want to finish even faster. “Sticks are just as good as logs,” he said. “Why bother chopping down a tree when I can gather a few branches and build my house in half the time?” Very quickly he was done, and he went back to watching for shapes in the clouds.

But the oldest piggy didn't select straw or sticks. He headed straight to town and bought as many bricks as he could. Then, he carefully laid them one by one. After several days of hard work, he had finished a fine house. It was sturdy and strong, with a tall chimney and even a cozy fireplace.

Late one afternoon, a hungry wolf passed by. He spotted the youngest piggy outside playing with the hedgehogs, and his stomach rumbled. “Looks like it’s time for dinner,” the wolf growled. “And my dinner is you!”

“Eep!” cried the little piggy. He raced inside his straw house and slammed the door.

“Little pig, little pig, let me come in,” said the wolf. His deep voice rattled the door. And for the first time, the little piggy wished his house was made of something other than straw.

“Not by the hair on my chinny-chin-chin!” he said, trembling.

“Then I’ll huff, and I’ll puff, and I’ll blow your house down!” cried the wolf. And he did!

What do you think the little pig felt when the wolf spotted him? Can you name two or three emotions? Have you ever had a similar reaction?

The youngest piggy was so frightened, he ran faster than his little legs had ever carried him before. He raced straight to his brother's house made of sticks, and once he was safely inside, they slammed the door together.

The wolf stomped up to the door. Now he could smell the two piggies inside, and his hunger doubled.

"Little pigs, little pigs, let me come in!" he snarled.

The piggies hugged each other tightly. "Not by the hairs on our chinny-chin-chins!" they said.

The wolf licked his lips. "Then I'll huff, and I'll puff, and I'll blow your house down!"

With just one blow, the house of sticks crumbled to the ground.

"EEEEP!" The two little pigs squealed with fright!

They just managed to slip through the wolf's eager paws and hurry down the path to their brother's brick house. He let them in at once, and they slammed the door.

Now the wolf could smell all three piggies, and he was hungrier than ever!

"Little pigs, little pigs, let me come in!" He banged upon the door.

"Not by the hairs on our chinny-chin-chins!" the oldest brother shouted.

"Then I'll huff, and I'll puff, and I'll blow your house down!" The wolf cackled. He had already blown down two houses. What was one more?

How do you think the oldest pig felt? Was he as scared as his younger brothers?

And so the wolf huffed!

And he puffed!

And he huffed and he puffed and he huffed and he puffed!

But no matter how hard or how long he blew, the sturdy brick house didn't topple.

It didn't even move an inch.

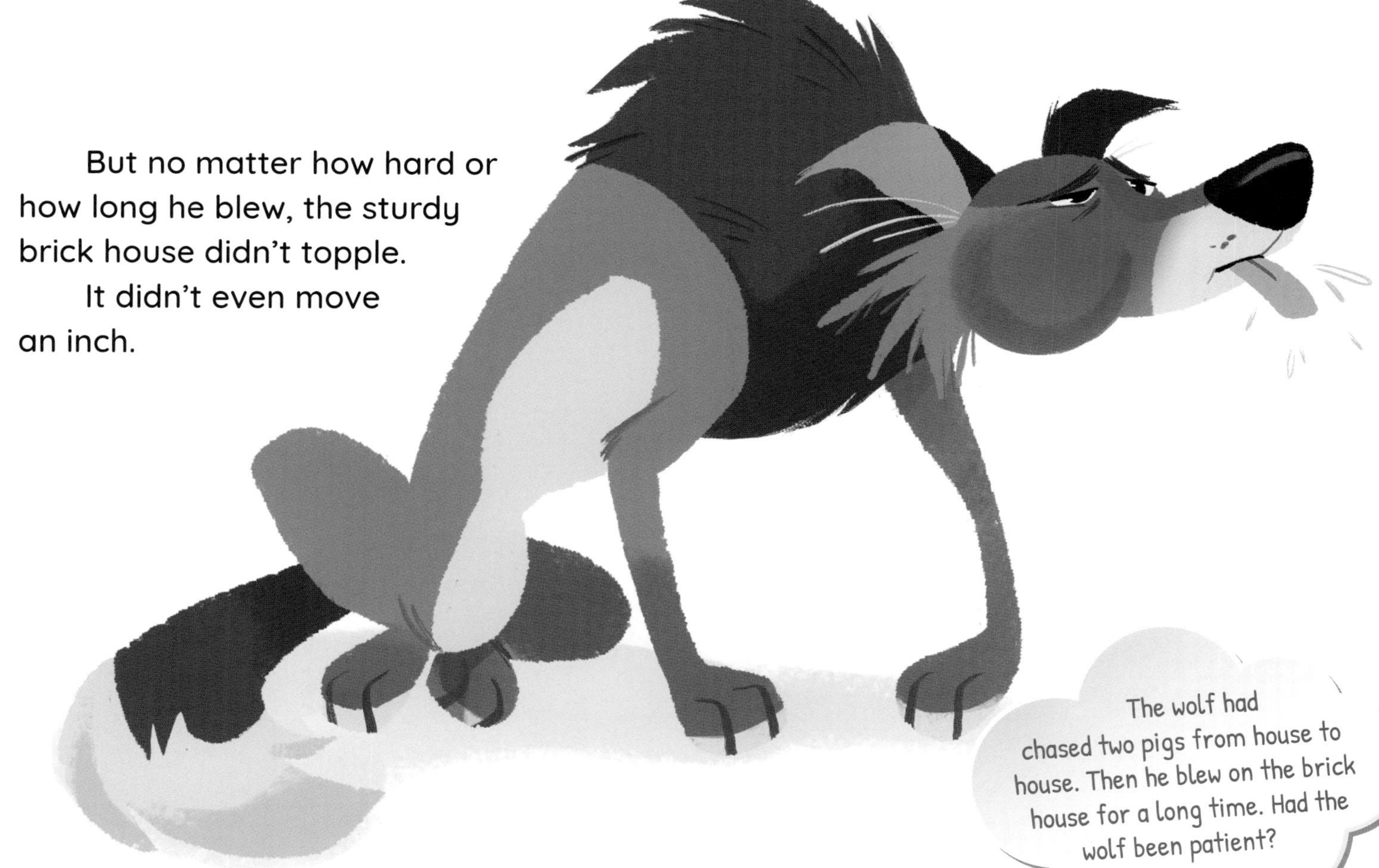

The wolf had chased two pigs from house to house. Then he blew on the brick house for a long time. Had the wolf been patient?

“No matter,” the wolf growled. “You piggies can’t stay in there forever. I shall wait for you to come out, and then I will gobble you up!”

“What are we going to do?” the two younger pigs asked, frightened. “He’s right, we can’t stay in here forever. And when we come out, he will devour us one by one.”

But their older brother just smiled as he always did. “I have an idea,” he said. “It will take patience. But I have a feeling patience is on our side.”

He gathered all the vegetables he had saved in his pantry. And then he simmered a delicious stew over a roaring fire in the fireplace.

Outside, the wolf sniffed the air. The delightful scent of both the stew and the pigs drifted past, and it drove him wild with hunger!

"Ooh, those pigs!" he cried. "I shall eat them this very second, in their very own stew!"

Without thinking, he clambered up the chimney, planning to drop down into the house and devour the pigs before they could escape.

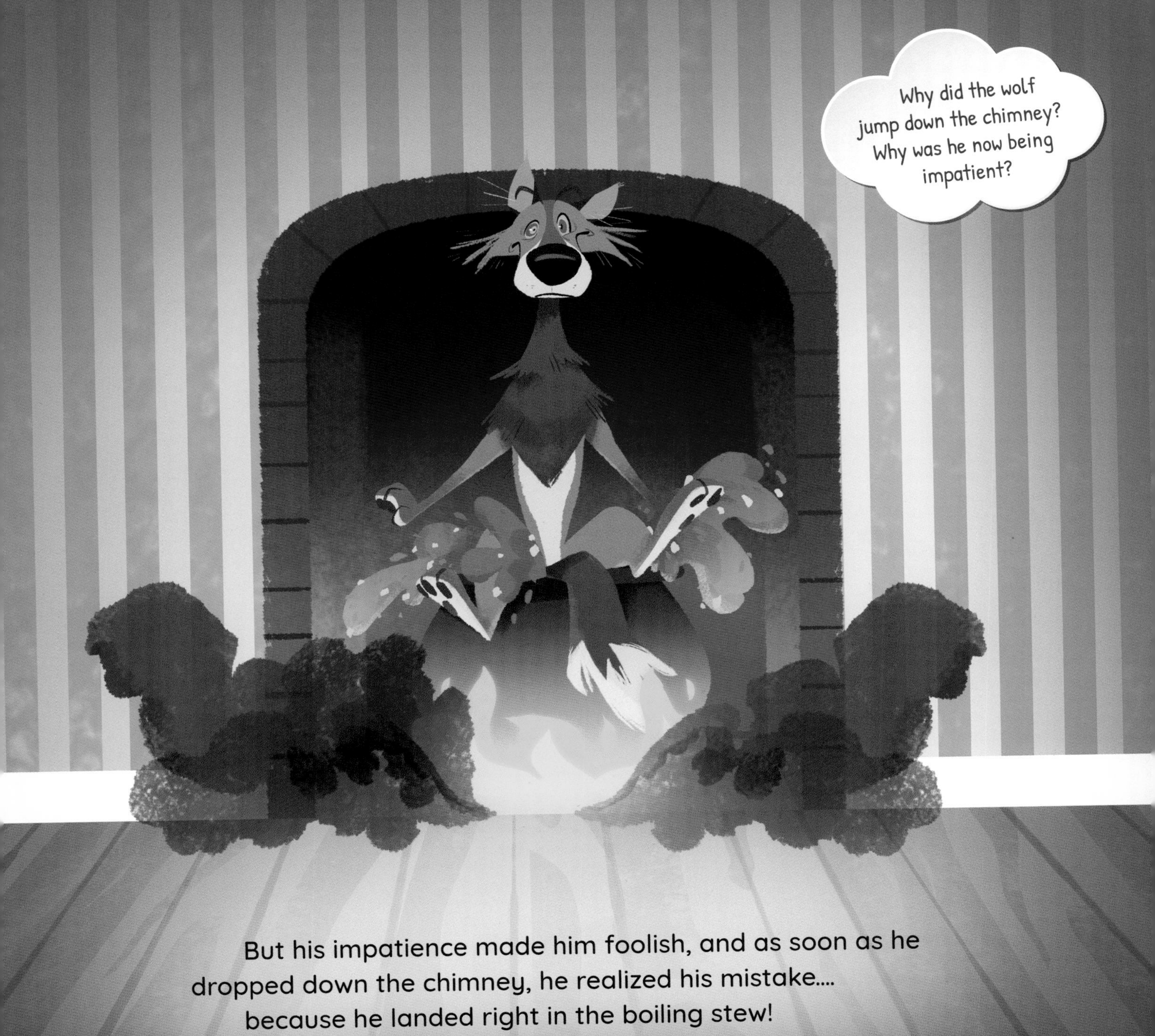

But his impatience made him foolish, and as soon as he dropped down the chimney, he realized his mistake.... because he landed right in the boiling stew!

“YEEEEOUCH!” cried the wolf.

The boiling stew burned his bottom so badly, he shot straight back up and out the chimney! Howling in pain, he ran away while holding his smoking tail, never to be seen again.

“Thank you, brother,” the two younger piggies said. “If it weren’t for you, we would be in that wolf’s stomach!”

“You’re welcome.” Their brother hugged them. “I’m glad you are safe. And I hope you’ve learned your lesson.”

“We have,” they replied. “We really have. We should have built our houses as you did, with sturdy bricks instead of sticks and straw.”

“But you know that using bricks takes time and patience,” their brother said. “Because sometimes, the things worth having are the things worth waiting for.”

The piggies nodded. “It’s never too late to start being patient,” they said. And they went right back to work!

What's something you once had to wait for? Was your patience worth it?

TO READ TOGETHER

What is patience?

Patience means waiting for something you want. It also means staying calm in situations you might not like. For example, you need patience to complete a puzzle, wait your turn in line, or learn a difficult skill. Doing a good job often means being patient!

What happens if I am impatient?

Sometimes you may not be patient. Maybe you really want to have something right now. Or you want to be the first one in line. Or you want to quickly finish something that you find boring. Don't worry! Patience takes practice. As you get older, it will get easier.

What can I do when I feel impatient?

If you feel impatient, let your parents or adults you trust know. Try to explain why it is important for you to get what you want. You can also imagine you have a balloon in your belly: Breathe in and blow it up five times. Put your hand on it to feel how it moves. Doing this will make you feel calmer. And it will help you be more patient too!

Be patient with impatience!

There are many ways to put your patience to work. Here are some ideas:

- Waiting for something doesn't mean having to do nothing. If you are riding on a long bus or car trip, play games like "I Spy." Or if you are waiting in a doctor's office, try remembering the lyrics to your favorite song or reading a book you brought from home. There are lots of little ways you can make waiting for something more fun!
- If you really want to say something in class, raise your hand and wait for your turn! If you want to be the first in line one day, talk to your teacher and explain why it is important to you.
- If something seems too difficult to complete, don't give up. Ask a grown-up for help and try again. Pretty soon, you'll be able to do it all on your own.
- Whenever you feel frustrated, try not to get angry. Instead, take a deep breath and count to five, or imagine you have that balloon in your belly!

You will see that if you practice, you will be a little bit more patient every day!

GUIDELINES FOR FAMILIES AND EDUCATORS

Before the ages of six or seven, children tend to be impatient very often, especially when they want something or a situation bores them. This is normal. During their first years of life, little ones have impulses that make them want to seek instant gratification. Later in life, they develop the ability to wait and bear with situations that they find unpleasant.

Showing them that we understand their wishes will help them feel secure. That does not mean always giving them what they want. We can acknowledge their wishes, even if we don't want to or cannot satisfy them. Feeling recognized by an adult will help soften the behaviors derived from impatience.

Here are some ways to encourage patience:

- Acknowledge that you understand their wishes saying things like: "I understand that you really want that toy, it looks really fun! Let's put it on your birthday list, and maybe you can get it then."

- Help them use their words to express the emotions that come from their actions. For example, try saying: "I know it is boring waiting at the doctor's office. You must feel frustrated and tired."

- Praise instances of patience when they happen, even if they are small. For instance, you can say: "I am so proud of you for being patient at the store! That was so grown-up of you!"

- Sit side by side as they complete a tedious task, like assembling a puzzle, writing a new word, or building a tower. Show them with your example why patience is worth it.

• If you ever lose patience, apologize to your child and ask them how they feel about your behavior. It is human to act impulsively out of frustration at times. Acknowledging our own failings shows them it is okay for them to do the same.

• Above all, remember that patience is built over the years and with your example. Be patient and compassionate of their behavior, and that will be the best lesson!

Helping children develop patience will make them more capable of sustaining situations where a reward is not immediate. It will facilitate teamwork and increase their attention span. These are tools that will be with them their whole life.

Eva Martínez is a teacher and family counselor. She is the author of two books about emotional education for children, and she is a regular contributor to educational magazines in her native Spain.

Enjoy the magic of fairy tales, and continue growing with more books in this series!

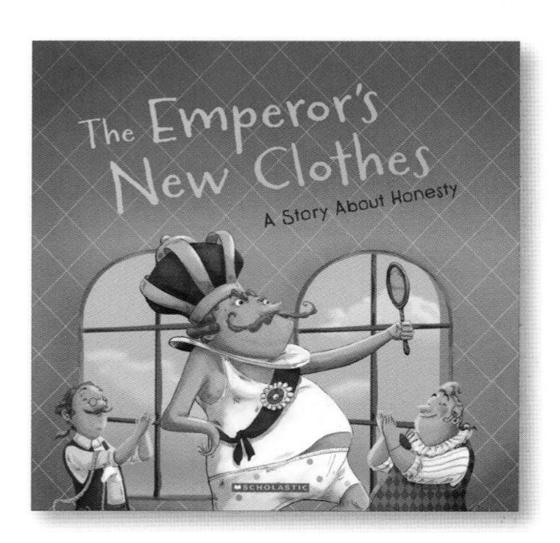

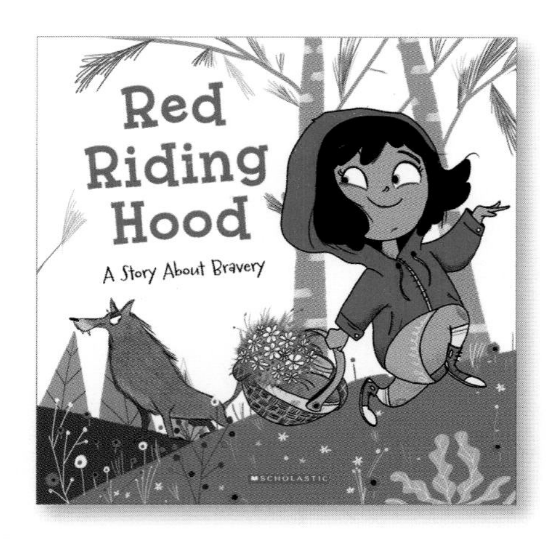